A Tree's Tale

story & pictures by Lark Carrier

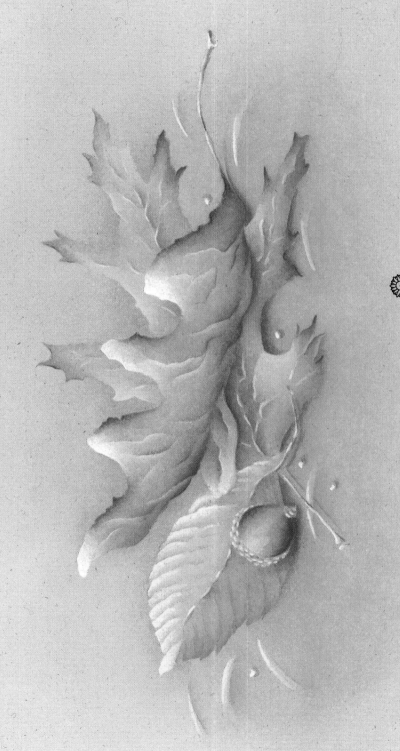

Dial Books for Young Readers · *New York*

In loving memory of my mother, Fern May,
and my father, Karlo Kemppainen

Special thanks to Nanepashemet, Director of the Wampanoag
Indian Program at the Plimoth Plantation, Massachusetts,
for the Wampanoag words Mai-Mehtug, as well as for his time.

Published by Dial Books for Young Readers
A Division of Penguin Books USA Inc.
375 Hudson Street • New York, New York 10014

Typography by Amelia Lau Carling
Printed in Hong Kong
First Edition
10 9 8 7 6 5 4 3 2

Library of Congress Cataloging in Publication Data
Carrier, Lark, 1947–
A tree's tale / story & pictures by Lark Carrier. — 1st ed.
p.   cm.
Summary: The huge, 400-year-old oak tree sees many
people come and go during the course of its life
as a path-tree to the inland forest.
ISBN 0-8037-1202-2 (trade). — ISBN 0-8037-1203-0 (lib. bdg.)
[1. Trees—Fiction.] I. Title.
PZ7.C23453Tr   1996   [E]—dc20   95-10855   CIP   AC

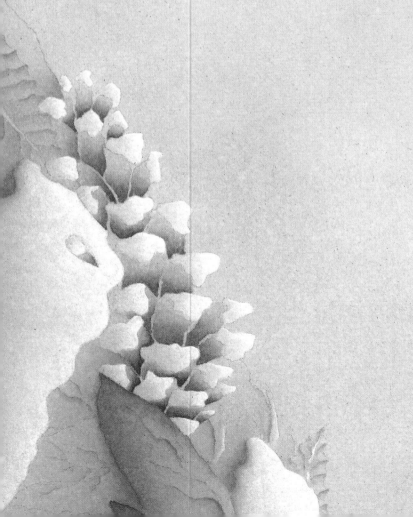

The art was rendered with watercolors on handmade paper.

There lives an oak tree that has not taken one step in over four hundred years, but what a journey it has had. . . . It all began when it was just a small acorn, fallen on the rich forest floor where the snow had melted away. Slowly it pushed up a sliver of green that swayed in the warm breeze rising from the sea below.

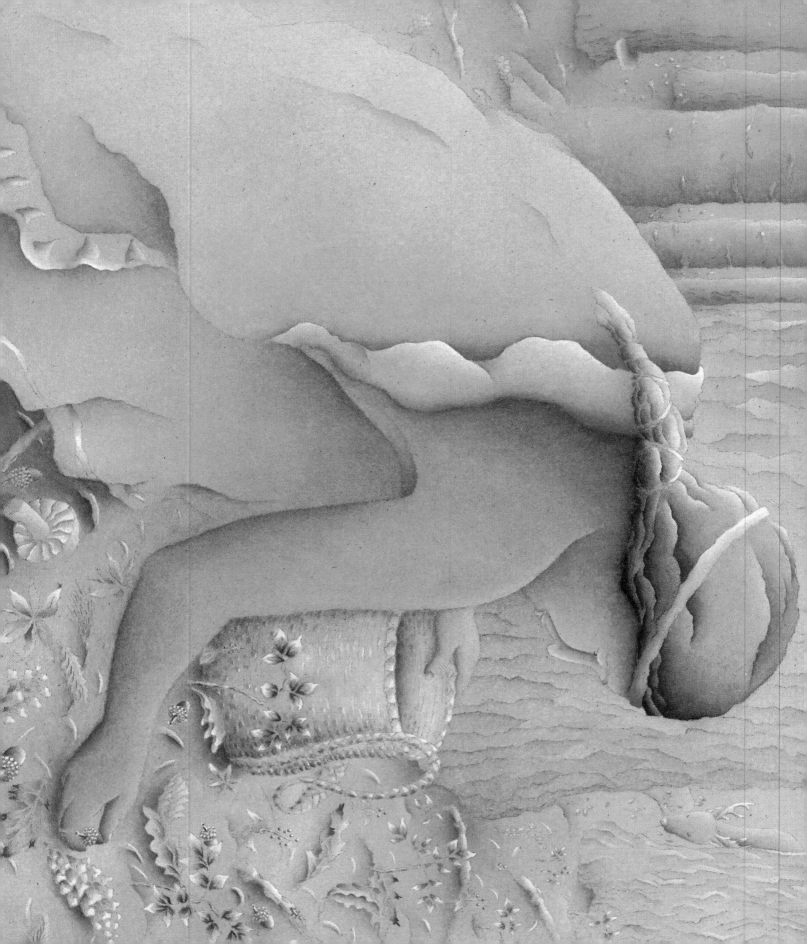

Long summer days made the seedling grow strong enough to survive the crushing moccasins of people gathering food. Autumn winds blanketed the seedling with colorful leaves, hiding it from hungry deer that pawed the ground in winter's cold.

Seasons passed, until the sapling was tall and willowy, and able to welcome nesting chickadees. As if in celebration, the sapling's leafy boughs and neighboring tree limbs rustled in the wind, bringing music to the hill.

One day two men silently moved through the forest like white-tailed deer. When they reached the young tree, their strong hands swiftly pinned it to the ground. It looked as though it would snap in two, but the men had chosen well, and the tender bark molded to the bend. With its crown pointing inland it became a guidepost to the west. And so it was named Mai-Mehtug, meaning "path-tree."

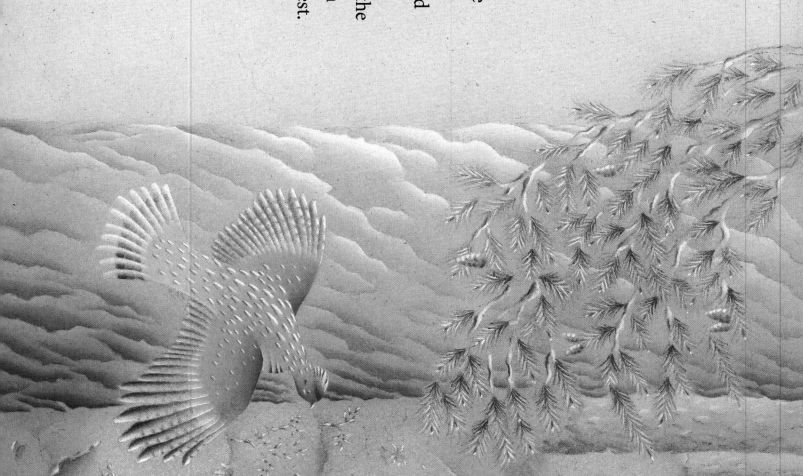

After many years the path-tree broke free from the bond that had given it its form. The people of the forest were always thankful to see Mai-Mehtug and never forgot to give it a gentle pat before following its westward direction. In time their feet wove an inland trail like a winding river through the dense woods.

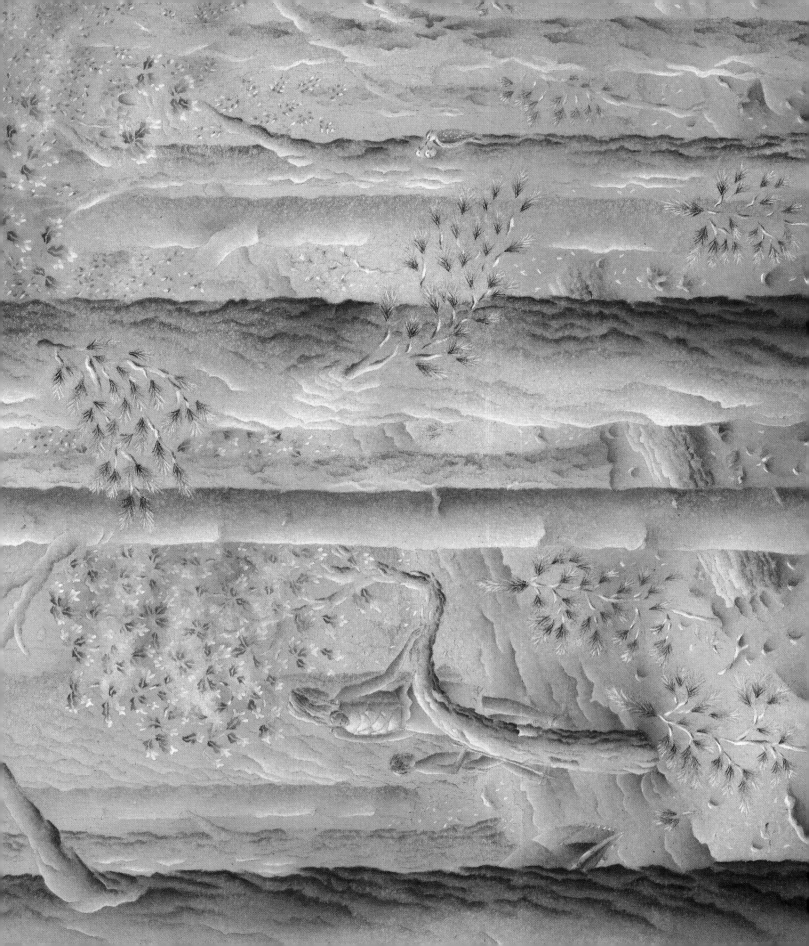

Then on a hot day in the mid-1600's, ships from across the sea sailed toward shore. They brought people with different dress and customs. They too traveled the inland trail, to hunt for food and cut timber to build their homes, but in their hurry no one stopped to pat the path-tree. And as the trail grew wider and the surrounding woods grew thinner, the music of rustling leaves began to disappear.

One day the blueberry bushes near the path-tree were crushed as a man lifted an ax and swung hard. As if struck by lightning, the path-tree's leaves shuddered helplessly in the wind while warm sap flowed from the wound in its trunk. But when the man raised his ax to strike again, a child cried, "Father, please stop! This could be a perfect swing-ing tree."

The man stepped back to look at the arched trunk. He then grinned and said, "Let's fetch some rope."

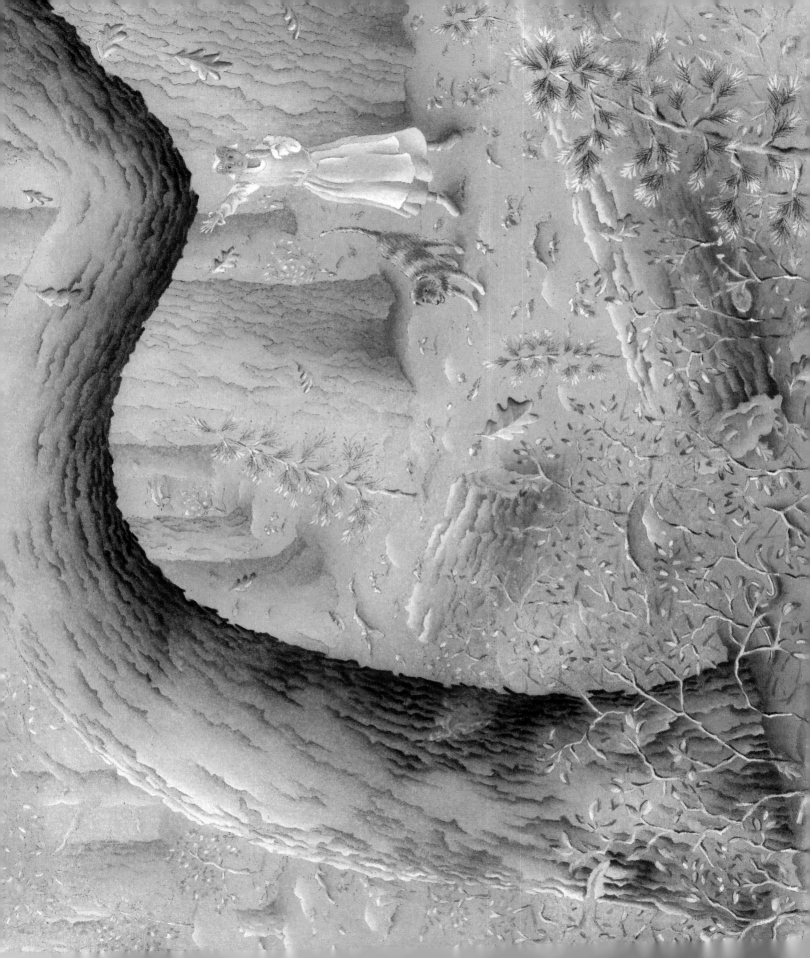

Soon all the village children climbed the hill to glide through the air. Their laughter mingled with the path-tree's rustling leaves, bringing a new music to the forest. When they had grown, their children came, and then theirs, until the thick ropes carved deep grooves as smooth as river rocks into the strong trunk.

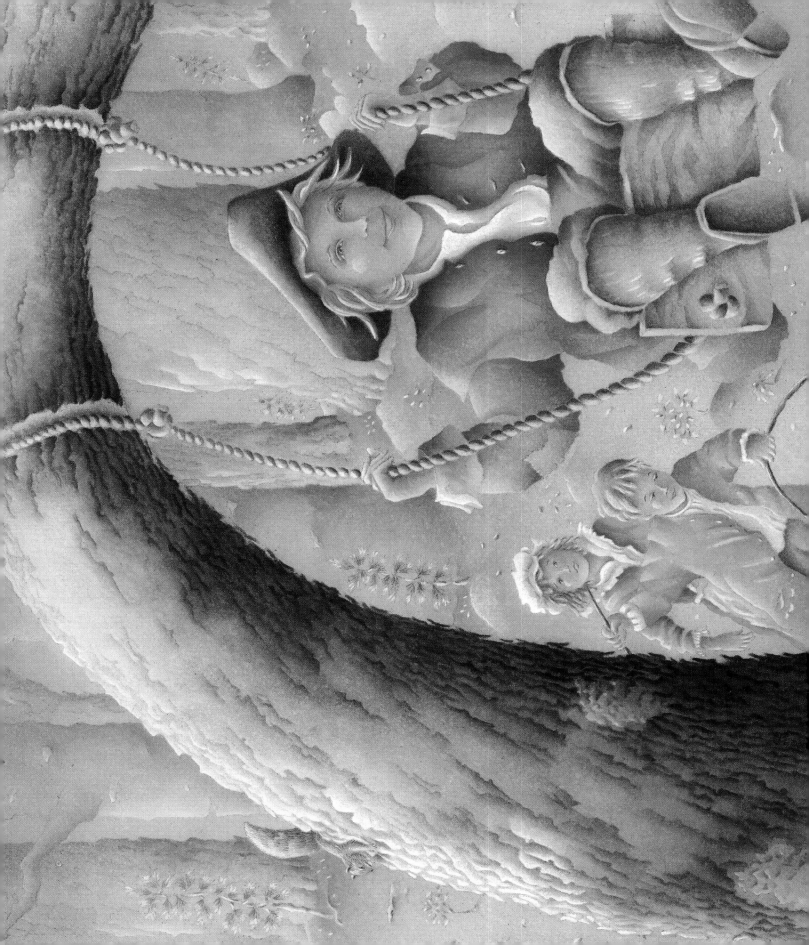

But by the late 1700's the village harbor and rich forest had attracted shipbuilders, and the docks were where the children wanted to play.

They cheered each arriving ship and waved good-bye to newly christened schooners sent out to sea, leaving the path-tree to stand alone.

One morning two men and a boy climbed the hill in search of new timber for the shipbuilders. As they approached the path-tree to chop it down, the boy shouted, "Wait! I could spot ships far out at sea if I were up there. Please don't take it down."

So once again children climbed the hill to the path-tree. There they took turns waving brightly colored flags to alert the villagers of arriving schooners. Over many years the gripping toes and fingers of the children were etched into the path-tree's bark like the pattern of busy woodpeckers.

When the tall, straight trees had been cut down, the shipbuilders moved away. Life at the harbor and on the hill faded, until a different people arrived, who cleared the land of the old tree stumps to plant fields of corn and rye. One day a farmer rested against the path-tree, wiped his brow, and said, "We'll fence this area for the cows. This big ol' crooked tree will be good for summer shade."

Though the path-tree remained standing, it was hard to be the lone survivor of a once dense forest. The cows' heavy hooves trampled its seedlings, the raging wind was unkind to its limbs, and the summer sun parched its leaves. And when the rains turned the ground into mud, its deep roots strained to keep its crown to the sky.

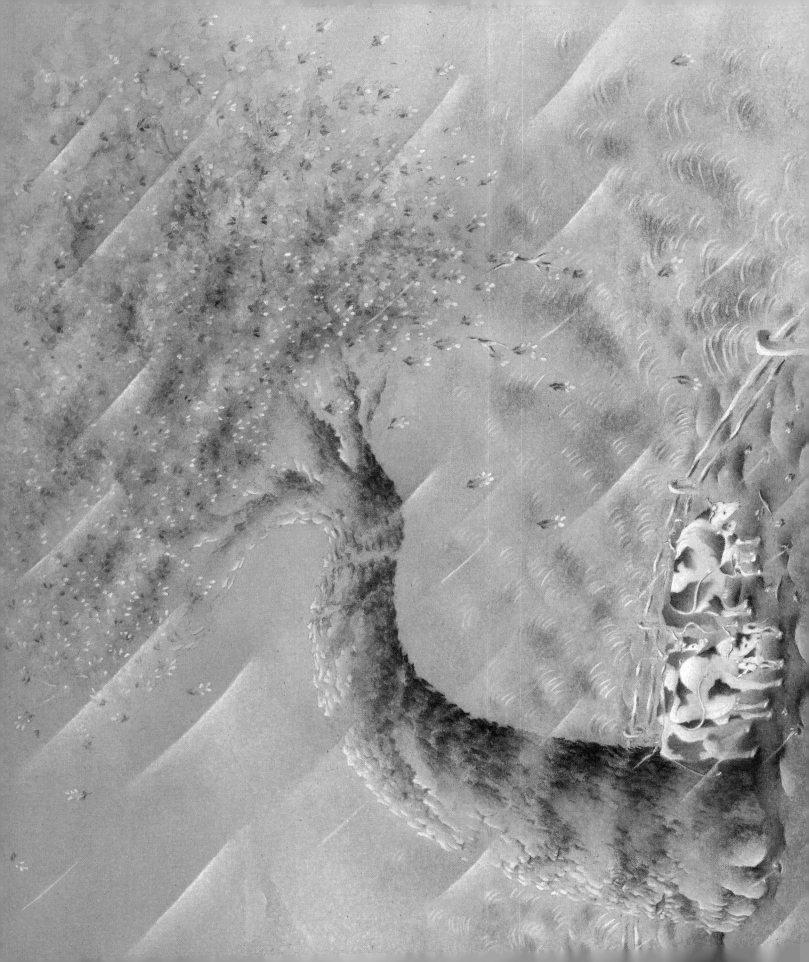

In time the land produced less as the soil tired. The fences were taken down and the cows freed to graze on wildflowers and strawberries that covered the unplowed fields. Soon many of the path-tree's seedlings took root and grew, and began to sway in the warm breeze from the sea below, just as the path-tree had so many years before.

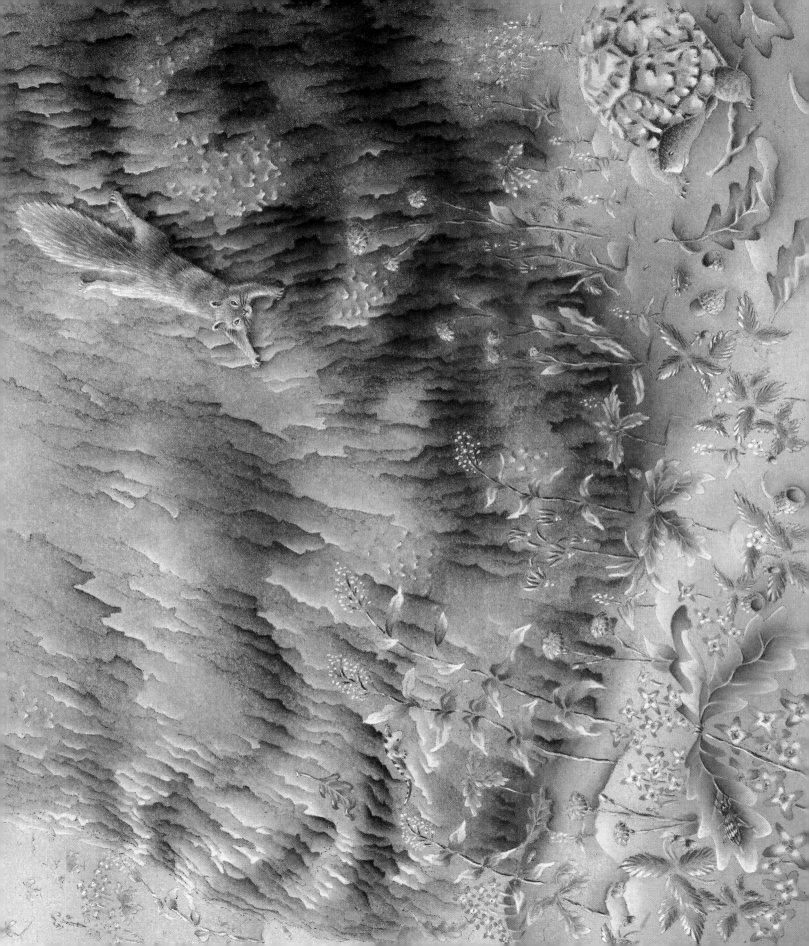

When the 1800's ended, the cows and farmers moved on to the rich valleys of the west. The hillside looked like a bear's thick winter coat, all new and shiny. The path-tree's crown was still the tallest, and caught the sea breeze. Some days— when a great horned owl landed on its trunk—it seemed as if a child had returned, as well as the music of laughter and rustling leaves.

Nearly one hundred years later the path-tree was magnificent, a giant of the forest. Then, like a flock of cawing crows, people once more swept onto the hillside. They wore bright-colored hats and drove noisy trucks. With harsh buzzing sounds the newcomers cut trees, dug pits, and built houses. When they were about to take down the path-tree, a man who had heard tales of the region shouted for them to stop. He then studied the path-tree's majestic arch, and with his gentle fingers traced the faint memories etched into its trunk. Finally, with a sigh and a smile, he patted the gash at the base of the path-tree and said, "I bet you've seen and heard a lot, Mai-Mehtug."

Later that summer the man and a large crowd returned with a wooden sign which read, "Mai-Mehtug: Path-Tree to the Inland Forest." As the man spoke of Mai-Mehtug's life, the crowd imagined the many people who had passed the path-tree with their different customs and dress. Children pointed, thinking they spotted ships far at sea. Others could almost feel the raging winds that had torn at the path-tree's boughs while it had stood alone. And when the wind rustled the path-tree's leaves as it swept up the hill, everyone thought they heard the children's laughter of long ago mingle with their own, in celebration of Mai-Mehtug's long journey.

Author's Note

There is little written about trees once used as trail markers in the dense forests, which at one time stretched from the Atlantic Ocean to the Midwest. Some historians maintain that this is because years ago trees bent for trail markers were so numerous, there was simply no need for documentation. Sadly, with the exception of a few that have been designated as landmarks in the Great Lakes region, most have died or been cut down.

When I was a child, my father spoke of the trail trees and I was fascinated. When I grew up and moved near Plymouth, Massachusetts—a place filled with history—I imagined a path-tree standing on a hill above the ocean, like a sentry watching all the changes being made to the land by the constant arrival of newcomers. What a tale this tree would be able to tell, I thought . . . and this is how I began my story.